W9-BMF-558

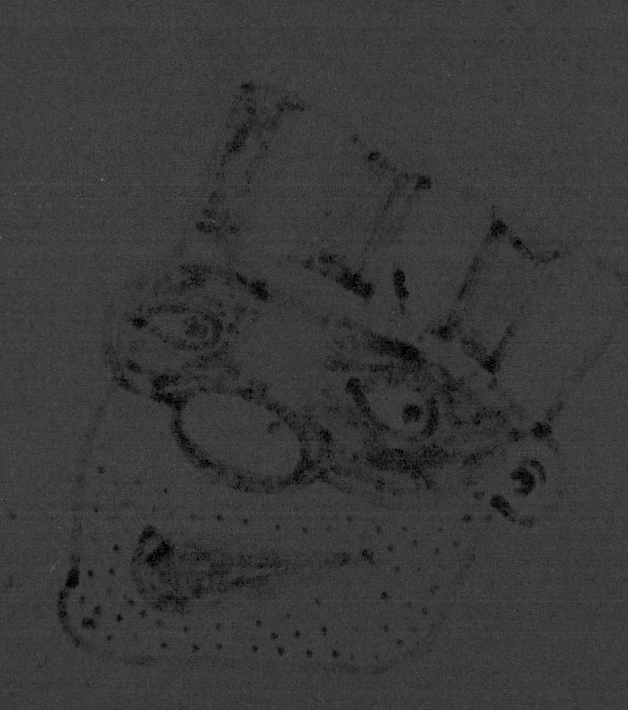

STAY OUT OF TROUBLE!

XO ALISON PAUL!
2010

SUNDAY LOVE

Alison Paul

Houghton Mifflin Books for Children
Houghton Mifflin Harcourt
Boston New York
2010

NO HEARTS WERE HARMED IN THE MAKING OF THIS BOOK.

Houghton Mifflin Books for Children is an imprint of Houghton Mifflin Harcourt Publishing Company.

www.hmhbooks.com

The text of this book is set in Cooper.
The illustrations are pen and ink and watercolor.

ISBN: 978-0-618-99184-6

Printed in Singapore
TWP 10 9 8 7 6 5 4 3 2 1

sniff
buzz
buzz

THE BIG HOUSE
scrape
grnnt
grnnt
CRUN

wheeWAAAA
chip,
chip,
chip
TUNNEL

POW!

GOOOOOOAL!

HALT!

HALT!

SPLISH
SPLASH!
tip toe
tip toe
tip toe
tip toe
tip toe

HALT!
I will not steal kisses
I will not steal kisses
I will not steal kisses
I will not steal kisses
I will not steal kisses
I will not steal kisses
HALT!

HALT!

HALT!

DING-

SNAP!

DONG

flap?

CRACK!

flap!
flap,

flap,
flap,

Hmph?

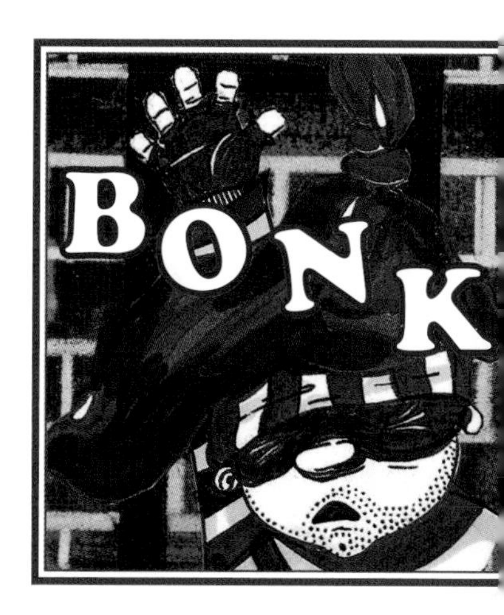

HALT!

WHOOSH!

CRASH!
BANG

FHOOMP!

Valentino's
ROMAN CANDLES
FIREWORKS SHOP

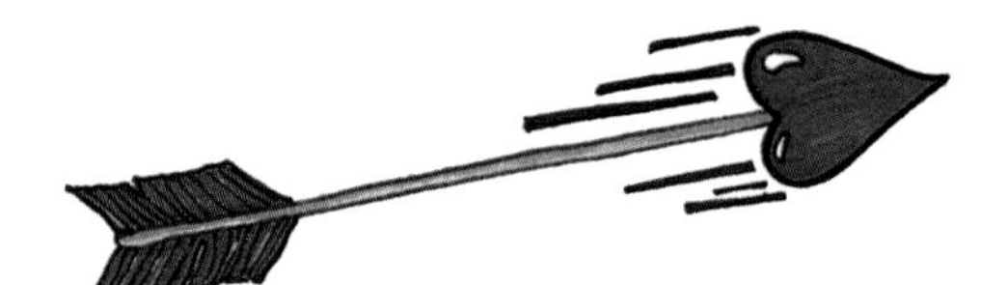

THWACK!

BULLFIGHT
TONIGHT

ONE WAY
POLICE STATI

BULLFIG
TONIG

¡olé!

THWACK!

The Valentine Times

VOL. V | SUNDAY, FEBRUARY 14, 2010 | LATE EDITION

FREE
ICE CREAM!

STOP BY THE ICE CREAM PARLOR FOR A *FREE SUNDAE!*

VALENTINE'S DAY ONLY!

HOME TEAM WINS!

FIRST VALENTINE'S CUP WIN

GOAL SCORED BY NEW PLAYER

2 14 2010

JAILBREAK!

Bruno the Burglar has broken out of the BIG HOUSE!

He is armed with a spoon—and probably dangerous!

MATADOR LIVES!

THE FAMOUS MATADOR VALENTINO HEART IS NOW RECOVERING FROM JUST A FLESH WOUND!

THE NEWSSTA
The Valentine Times
JAIL BREAK!

Valentino's

KA-BOOM!

KABOOM!

ice cream
FREE SUNDAES
VALENTINE'S DAY ONLY!

TAP
TAP

SLAM

flap

flap

THE
Shh!
END